Is Gray Eagle Stupid?

"Liz, guess what?" Jessica said. "I met a storyteller. He knows tons of great stories from long ago. And he gave me an eagle feather!" She held it up, then turned to Ann. "Do you know Gray Eagle?"

"He's my grandfather," Ann said.

"Really?" Jessica said. "That's excellent."

"If you say so," Ann said. "He's just a stupid old man. I don't pay attention to him. All he's interested in is Indians. *Bo*-ring."

Jessica felt herself getting angry. "I think you're the one who's stupid," she told Ann.

"Me? You don't know anything," Ann yelled. "Just mind your own business." She stomped off, looking furious.

Jessic_____ ___ __ Elizabeth. "What's wrong _____

D1401661

Bantam Skylark Books in the
SWEET VALLEY KIDS series

SWEET VALLEY KIDS

THE TWINS' BIG POW-WOW

Written by
Molly Mia Stewart

Created by
FRANCINE PASCAL

Illustrated by
Ying-Hwa Hu

A BANTAM SKYLARK BOOK ®
NEW YORK·TORONTO·LONDON·SYDNEY·AUCKLAND

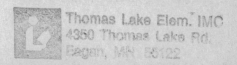

RL 2, 005-008

THE TWINS' BIG POW-WOW
A Bantam Skylark Book / November 1993

Sweet Valley High® and Sweet Valley Kids are
trademarks of Francine Pascal

Conceived by Francine Pascal

Produced by Daniel Weiss Associates, Inc.
33 West 17th Street
New York, NY 10011

Cover art by Susan Tang

Skylark Books is a registered trademark of Bantam Books, a
division of Bantam Doubleday Dell Publishing Group, Inc.
Registered in U.S. Patent and Trademark Office and elsewhere.

ISBN: 0-553-48098-7

Published simultaneously in the United States and Canada

Bantam Books are published by Bantam Books, a division of Bantam
Doubleday Dell Publishing Group, Inc. Its trademark, consisting of the
words "Bantam Books" and the portrayal of a rooster, is Registered in
U.S. Patent and Trademark Office and in other countries. Marca
Registrada. Bantam Books, 1540 Broadway, New York, New York 10036.

PRINTED IN THE UNITED STATES OF AMERICA

OPM   0 9 8 7 6 5 4 3 2 1

CHAPTER 1

On the Road

"I'll clear the table," Elizabeth Wakefield said.

"I'll help," said her twin sister, Jessica.

"Me too," Steven said. He was their older brother.

Elizabeth, Jessica, and Steven all jumped up from the dining-room table. The three of them had just finished Thanksgiving dinner. But their father was still drinking his coffee, and their mother was still eating her pumpkin pie.

"That was probably the fastest Thanksgiving dinner ever," Mr. Wakefield said.

Mrs. Wakefield laughed. "Maybe we set a world's record." She got up from the table and started piling the dessert plates on top of each other.

The Wakefields were going on vacation. They were going to spend the rest of their four-day weekend at Fort Mojave, an Indian reservation. The reservation was on the Colorado River, near the southwestern corner of Nevada. Elizabeth and Jessica had found it in the atlas at least a dozen times over the past week. To get to the reservation, the Wakefields were going to drive about five hours. Part of the trip was across the Mojave Desert. Elizabeth, Jessica, and Steven couldn't wait to get on the road.

Jessica grabbed a glass. Elizabeth snatched up the milk. They both reached for the pie plate at the same time.

Elizabeth smiled at Jessica as she let go.

Jessica and Elizabeth often did things at the same time. That was because Elizabeth and Jessica were *identical* twins. The two girls looked exactly alike. Both had blue-green eyes and long blond hair with bangs. When they wore matching outfits, the only way to tell them apart was by looking at the name bracelets they always wore.

But just because they looked the same on the outside didn't mean the twins were the same on the inside. Elizabeth loved animals, the woods, and muddy soccer games. Jessica liked *stuffed* animals, her dollhouse, and ladylike tea parties. She enjoyed wearing pretty clothes, and she didn't like getting them dirty.

Despite their differences, Elizabeth and Jessica agreed that being twins was special. They shared a bedroom, toys, and secrets. They were going to be best friends forever.

"We're almost finished here," Mrs. Wakefield said, coming through the kitchen door and looking at what was left on the dining-room table. "Why don't you kids go upstairs and finish packing?"

Jessica, Elizabeth, and Steven ran up to the second floor. When the twins got to their room, Elizabeth put her bath kit in her suitcase and snapped it closed. She had also packed jeans, T-shirts, and a sweatshirt. Elizabeth had saved room in her suitcase for souvenirs.

"Would you help me?" Jessica asked.

"Sure," Elizabeth said. But when she saw Jessica's suitcase, she frowned. It overflowed with jeans and T-shirts—plus dressy shoes, tights, and hair ribbons.

4

Jessica had even packed her brand-new party dress.

"Are you sure you want all this stuff?" Elizabeth asked.

"I don't want it," Jessica said. "I *need* it. We might go to a party."

"What if it gets cold?" Elizabeth asked.

"I don't have room for a sweatshirt," Jessica said.

"I'll put it with my things," Elizabeth offered.

Jessica grinned. "Thanks."

"OK," Elizabeth said, looking at her sister's suitcase again. "I'll push. You snap." Working together, Jessica and Elizabeth managed to fasten Jessica's suitcase.

"Don't forget your money," Elizabeth said.

"I already have it in my purse," Jessica said. She picked up her pink satin

change purse and tied the string ends to her belt loop.

Mr. and Mrs. Wakefield had given them and Steven ten dollars each to spend at the reservation. Jessica already knew she wanted to buy a turquoise ring with her money. Turquoise was a kind of blue stone, and Jessica thought it was beautiful.

Elizabeth and Jessica carried their suitcases downstairs and out to the driveway. Mr. Wakefield put them in the back of the station wagon with all the other bags. Then Jessica and Elizabeth climbed into the backseat and fastened their seat belts. When everyone was settled, Mr. Wakefield started the car and drove toward the highway.

Jessica and Elizabeth bounced up and down in their seats.

"Cut it out," Steven said. He was sit-

7

ting next to them. "We haven't even left Sweet Valley yet."

"I can't help it," Jessica said.

"Me neither," Elizabeth said. "I really want to meet some Indians. I wonder if they'll be like the ones on TV." Jessica and Elizabeth loved to watch old cowboy-and-Indian movies on television.

"I want to see a tepee," Jessica said.

"And a rain dance," Elizabeth said.

Steven shook his head. "You guys are crazy."

"What do you mean?" Elizabeth asked.

"You wouldn't understand," Steven said.

"The girls are curious," Mr. Wakefield told Steven as he looked at them from the rearview mirror. "Why don't you tell us all about what you learned in school?" Steven's class had been studying early American history.

8

"Well, all right." Steven sighed. "Real-life Indians aren't like the ones in movies. They aren't even *called* Indians. They like to be called Native Americans."

"If they're not Indians," Jessica asked, "how come we call them Indians?"

"When Christopher Columbus landed in America," Steven explained, "he thought he was in India! So he called the Native Americans 'Indians'. But he was wrong."

Mrs. Wakefield was looking at a road map. "I think we missed our turn," she told Mr. Wakefield.

"I hope we don't get as lost as Columbus did," Mr. Wakefield said.

"We might end up in China," Steven said.

"Or Mars," Elizabeth added, laughing. She and Jessica exchanged excited looks. They were on their way at last.

CHAPTER 2

Exploring

Jessica opened her eyes and smiled. She unzipped her sleeping bag and sat up. "Liz, it's morning!"

"That's nice," Elizabeth mumbled as she rolled over.

Jessica reached over and tickled her sister until she woke up. As soon as her eyes were open, Elizabeth broke into a grin. "It's morning!"

Jessica giggled. "I just told you that."

Elizabeth and Jessica had spent the night in their new two-person tent. Mrs. Wakefield had bought it for the trip. It was made out of bright-green material and was the perfect size for them. Steven had his own tent, and so did their parents.

The Wakefields had arrived at the reservation late the night before. Everyone had been too tired to look around. Now Elizabeth and Jessica couldn't wait to go exploring. They pulled on their clothes and hurried outside.

Mr. Wakefield was sitting at a picnic table in front of the tents. "Good morning, girls. Hurry up and brush your teeth. It's almost time for breakfast."

The twins grabbed their bath kits and ran toward the visitors' bathrooms. As Jessica brushed her teeth, she thought about what she knew about the reservation. Elizabeth and Jessica had read a book about Fort

Mojave in the car the evening before.

Jessica had learned that Fort Mojave was over a hundred years old. She had found out it was big—more than 250,000 acres. Mr. Wakefield had said that their whole yard back home was less than half an acre.

Jessica smiled at her reflection. She couldn't wait to go see everything on the reservation and learn even more.

Breakfast was served at a long outdoor table. Dozens of visitors were already sitting around it. A few Native Americans were waiting to eat, too. The Wakefields found seats. Soon big bowls of food were passed down from one end of the table to the other.

Steven took a bowl and frowned. "I don't know about this," he said, looking at the food. "Mom, do you know what this is?"

Mrs. Wakefield peeked into the bowl. "Looks like fish."

"Fish?" Steven asked. "For breakfast? Yuck! Where are the eggs?"

A Native American man sitting nearby spoke up. "At every meal here you'll be offered some traditional Native American foods. That includes things like beans, maize—what you call corn—pumpkins, sunflower seeds, and fish. But don't worry. We also serve food our guests are more accustomed to eating. So hang on. The eggs should be coming."

Mr. Wakefield smiled at the man. He introduced himself and the rest of the family.

"I'm Henry," the man said. "Welcome to Fort Mojave."

"Your name is Henry?" a little boy sitting nearby asked. "I thought you'd have a special Indian name."

"Shh," said the boy's mother. "It's not polite to be so nosy."

Henry smiled. "No problem. I do have another name. It's Red Sand. You can call me whichever one you want."

"I like Red Sand," the little boy said. "My name's Donny."

"I'm Patty Kale," his mother said. "I was excited to come here because I make clay pots back in Santa Barbara. I love the traditional Mojave Indian designs."

As they ate, Henry told them about the available activities on the reservation. There was tons to do. You could learn how to make baskets and beaded jewelry, go to demonstrations of Native American storytelling and herbal medicine, and learn how to ride a horse.

"What should we do first?" Elizabeth asked Jessica once breakfast was over.

Jessica shrugged. "Don't forget about the gift shop." She looked around. There were several tan adobe buildings on the reservation, but what she could see the most of was open land. "Where is everybody?" she added. "Aren't there any Native American *kids* on this reservation?"

"More than two thousand people live here," Elizabeth said. That had been in the book, too.

"There used to be more," Steven said. "Lots more."

Elizabeth nodded. "White people killed them."

"But *how* did they kill them?" someone spoke up behind them.

Jessica, Elizabeth, and Steven spun around. A Native American boy about Steven's age was standing behind them.

"The cowboys had guns," Steven

15

said. "The Indians only had bows and arrows."

The boy shook his head. "Most of my ancestors didn't die in battles with white men. They died of diseases the Europeans carried," he said. "My people had never been exposed to these diseases, so they didn't how to deal with them."

"I didn't know that," Steven said.

Jessica and Elizabeth exchanged smiles. They were happy *somebody* knew more about Native Americans than Steven.

"I'm Brave Wolf," the boy said.

Jessica, Elizabeth, and Steven introduced themselves.

"Have you met Water Lily?" Brave Wolf asked Jessica and Elizabeth. They shook their heads.

Brave Wolf frowned. "She was supposed to be at breakfast. Why don't you look for her in the stable? It's over there." He pointed to a low wooden building with a closed ring for riding in back of it.

"Let's go meet Water Lily," Jessica said. She grabbed Elizabeth's hand and they ran off.

CHAPTER 3

Starfire

Elizabeth and Jessica opened the door to the stable. They had never seen a horse up close before. And they didn't see just one. Each stall had a horse in it, bringing the total to ten horses.

"Do you hear all of them munching hay?" Elizabeth asked. Jessica nodded. "And I smell them, too." She took a step back. "I didn't know horses were so big and smelly."

"I like the smell," Elizabeth said. She took an enormous breath. "Kind of like donkeys, huh?"

"Right," Jessica said. "But donkeys are a lot smaller." They had both ridden donkeys on a trip to the Grand Canyon. Jessica hadn't liked the way they smelled either.

Elizabeth shrugged her shoulders and went to the horse in the first stall. "I think it smells great in here."

"You're weird," Jessica said.

The mare in the first stall dropped her head over the stall door and nudged Elizabeth's shoulder with her muzzle. "Oh, you're so beautiful," Elizabeth said as she reached up and rubbed the horse's soft nose. The horse was black, with a white star on its head. Elizabeth could feel the horse's breath on her cheek.

"Her name's Starfire," a girl's voice said.

Elizabeth and Jessica both turned and

saw a Native American girl standing by a stall at the other end of the stable.

"Are you Water Lily?" Jessica asked.

"Yes," the girl said, frowning. "But call me Ann. Almost everyone does." Ann was wearing jeans and a striped T-shirt. Her hair was cut short.

"I'm Elizabeth," Elizabeth said. "And this is my sister, Jessica."

"How come you aren't wearing any beads?" Jessica asked Ann. "Or any turquoise?"

Elizabeth knew why Jessica had asked that question. Ann didn't look like the Native American girls in movies. She was wearing the same kind of clothes the twins and their friends at Sweet Valley Elementary School wore.

"All Native Americans don't wear that junk," Ann said.

"It's not junk," Jessica said. "I love it. I'm going to buy a turquoise ring as soon as I find the gift shop."

"You can buy every single one, for all I care," Ann said angrily.

Elizabeth decided to change the subject. "Is it OK to look at the horses?"

"Sure," Ann said. "I'll show you around."

Ann led the twins around the stable. She introduced them to Spright, Amber, Marvel, and all the other horses.

"Can you ride bareback?" Elizabeth asked.

Ann shook her head. "It's too hard. I haven't been riding long at all. But I'd like to learn to ride bareback someday."

"Starfire's my favorite," Elizabeth announced when Ann finished showing them around.

"Amber's mine," Ann said. "I love her golden color."

"I don't have a favorite," Jessica said.

"You can take riding lessons every morning and afternoon," Ann told them. "On Sundays there's a competition for kids who took lessons during their stay here. If you want to enter, I can help you practice."

Elizabeth's eyes widened. "That sounds great. Only, we've never ridden horses before," she said.

"Then you'll have to learn," Ann told her. "You can start this morning. It's almost time for the lesson."

Elizabeth smiled. "I'm ready!"

CHAPTER 4

Gray Eagle

"Come on," Jessica pleaded. "Let's go to the gift shop instead." She didn't want to ride any horse or enter any competition. All she wanted to do was buy a turquoise ring.

"I'm staying here," Elizabeth said.

"How come?" Jessica wanted to know.

"Don't you want to learn to ride?" Elizabeth asked.

"No, I don't," Jessica said. "Anyway, we can't learn to ride in a just a few days."

Elizabeth shrugged her shoulders. "So?"

"So I want to go to the gift shop," Jessica said.

Ann came back. She was carrying a bunch of big, small, and medium-sized brushes. "Do you want to help me groom Starfire?" she asked. "We have time."

"Yes," Elizabeth said. She nodded. "There's a lot to do when you have a horse."

"I'll just watch," Jessica said, crossing her arms.

Ann let herself into Starfire's stall. Elizabeth followed. As Elizabeth came in, the mare nudged her with her muzzle again.

Ann laughed. "She likes you!"

Elizabeth grinned. Ann showed her all of the different brushes, and explained about not standing right in back of Starfire's rear hooves.

"Even a gentle horse like Starfire can get nervous if you're in back of her and she can't see you," she explained. Then Elizabeth started to help Ann groom the horse.

Jessica stood on one foot and then the other. She sighed. Elizabeth seemed to have forgotten about going to the gift shop. Jessica was getting bored waiting for her.

"I'm leaving now," Jessica called to the other girls.

Elizabeth didn't even look up. "See you later."

Jessica walked out into the sunshine. After wandering around for a few minutes, she found Mr. and Mrs. Wakefield. They were listening to a Native American woman tell them about the different plants that grew in the area.

Jessica listened for a bit, then lost interest. She walked on. Soon she found Steven. Brave Wolf was teaching him how to make a fire without matches.

"Do you want to learn, too?" Brave Wolf offered.

"No," Jessica said. "I'm looking for the gift shop."

Brave Wolf pointed to a building in the distance. "It's in there."

"Thanks." Jessica ran across the courtyard and pushed open the gift shop's door. Inside, a Native American woman was sitting behind a counter. She looked up when the bell on the door jingled. "Hello," said the woman.

"Hi," Jessica said. She glanced around and noticed strings of colorful beads hanging from a doorway to the left. People were talking inside, but

Jessica didn't investigate. She had too much to look at.

The shop was packed with jewelry. Bracelets, rings, necklaces, and earrings hung from display stands. There were also rugs, pottery, baskets, clothes, fabric, beads, and postcards. Jessica's head was spinning. How would she ever decide what to buy? Then she reminded herself that she wanted a ring. After a few difficult minutes, she picked one out.

"Should I put it in a box?" the woman asked.

Jessica shook her head. "No, thank you. I want to wear it."

The woman smiled and handed Jessica the ring. Jessica got out her pink satin purse and gave the woman her ten-dollar bill.

Just then an old man walked into the

shop. "Good morning, Clear Creek," he said as he passed by.

"Good morning, Gray Eagle," the woman said. "There's a large group waiting for you."

The man smiled and pushed through the hanging beads in a doorway. There was sudden quiet in the other room. Clear Creek handed Jessica three dollars.

"Wow, I still have money left?" Jessica said. "That means I can get something else."

She started to look around again. But then she heard a deep, soft voice begin to speak. It was a beautiful voice. She crept toward the beads, listening.

"It's story hour," Clear Creek explained. "Why don't you go in?"

Jessica nodded. "I'll be back."

She walked through the beads and into the next room. More than a dozen people were seated on chairs. They faced Gray Eagle. Jessica didn't see an empty seat, so she crept to the front of the crowd and sat down on the floor, by Gray Eagle's feet. Jessica thought Gray Eagle looked as if he was a thousand years old. His face was covered with wrinkles.

Gray Eagle smiled at Jessica. From behind his back, he pulled out a colorful feather and handed it to her.

"Thank you," Jessica whispered as she accepted it.

"I am storyteller to the Mojave," Gray Eagle said, looking out at the room full of people. "Native Americas used to teach their children by telling them stories. Imagine! No school."

A few kids in the audience cheered.

"Usually," Gray Eagle went on, "the storytellers, who were also teachers, were elderly."

"Like you!" Jessica said.

"Like me," Gray Eagle agreed. "The Mojave believe only one man in the tribe can be a storyteller. Before he dies, a storyteller gives his stories to his son."

"Can girls tell stories?" Jessica asked.

Gray Eagle smiled. "My granddaughter says girls can do anything boys can do. If she says so, it must be true.

"The story I am about to tell you was first dreamed by a person who has now passed from this world. I will tell his story for his children and grandchildren. It is a story without time."

CHAPTER 5

An Ancient Story

"**O**nce upon a time," Gray Eagle began, "there lived a girl who was not happy with simple things. She was called Falling Leaves.

"Falling Leaves was the proper age to marry. But even though many of the men in the village wished to marry her, she would not accept any of them. Some were too fat, some were too thin; some were too tall, some were too short.

"One night a handsome stranger came to the girl's home. 'I have come to take you as my wife,' he told her.

"Falling Leaves's mother begged her not to go with the stranger, but the girl loved the man's fancy yellow and black clothes. She agreed to go with him. According to the customs of the time, that meant they were married."

"When I get married," Jessica interrupted, "I'm going to wear a long white dress and have a big party."

"So, you want fancy things just like Falling Leaves?" Gray Eagle asked Jessica.

Jessica nodded.

"You have spoken too soon, child," Gray Eagle said. "Wait and see what happens to Falling Leaves."

"The man led his new bride a long way away," Gray Eagle continued. "They walked far to a river and down a steep bank. Finally the man showed Falling Leaves a house. 'We will live here,' the man said. Then he offered Falling Leaves a dress. It was the fanciest dress she had ever seen. It was yellow and black, just like the clothes her husband wore. But Falling Leaves was afraid of the dress. It smelled of snakes. And, in case you don't know, snakes smell terrible.

" 'I won't wear it,' Falling Leaves said.

"Her husband was angry. He left the house, but he ordered Falling Leaves to stay inside. She was frightened and began to cry. Falling Leaves thought of her mother's house and wished she were back home. The simple home of her childhood now seemed the most wonderful place in the world to her.

"Just then, a huge snake with yellow and black skin entered the house from an open window. Falling Leaves screamed and ran outside. But she couldn't step off the porch because hundreds of snakes surrounded the house. That's when she knew her husband was a snake himself. He was just pretending to be a person. Falling Leaves guessed that if she put on the beautiful dress he had offered her, she would become a snake, too."

Jessica leaned forward with her mouth open.

"That night, Falling Leaves's grandfather appeared to her in a dream. He told her that she must get up and run to the distant cliffs. The snakes she had seen outside were asleep. She must not look back until she reached the top of the cliffs.

"Falling Leaves woke up and ran as fast as she could. As she went, she heard her husband call to her.

"'Come back and I will give you beautiful gifts,' he said.

"But Falling Leaves kept running. She ran to the cliffs and didn't stop until she was safe in her own village.

"Not long after that, Falling Leaves married a simple man with a good heart, and they lived happily ever after."

"Wow," Jessica whispered when the story was over. She fiddled with the turquoise ring on her finger. Then and there, Jessica decided not to go back to the gift shop. She was happy with the ring and the feather Gray Eagle had given her. She didn't need any more souvenirs.

But Jessica *did* want to hear more of

Gray Eagle's stories. Gray Eagle had said listening to stories was how Native American children used to learn—and Jessica wanted to learn lots more about the Mojave.

CHAPTER 6

Computers and Rain Dances

"Tell me more about the race," Elizabeth said to Ann as they brushed down Starfire.

Ann shook her head. "It's not a race. It's a competition. Whoever has the best riding skills wins. The judges watch your seat, your posture, how you hold the reins. Stuff like that."

"Sounds hard," Elizabeth said.

"It is," Ann agreed. "There's a boy named Luke visiting the reservation who's been taking riding lessons for months. But I think I can beat him."

"I hope I win," Elizabeth said.

Ann laughed. "You haven't even had your first lesson yet."

Elizabeth smiled. "Maybe I'll learn fast."

"Well, I hope *I* win," Ann said. "My brother, Brave Wolf, says I'm no good with horses. That makes me so mad! He thinks he's a much better rider. I'm always trying to prove he's wrong."

"Brave Wolf is your brother?" Elizabeth asked.

Ann nodded. "Did you meet him?"

"Yes," Elizabeth said. She put down one brush and picked up another. "Have you ever won the competition?"

"Twice," Ann said. "But that's nothing compared to my brother. He's won so many competitions, Mom and Dad made him stop entering."

41

"Are your parents good with horses?" Elizabeth asked.

"They're OK," Ann said. "But they don't ride much anymore. They aren't on the reservation a lot during the day. Both of them work in Needles. That's a town near here. My grandfather watches me and Brave Wolf during the day while they're gone."

"That's great," Elizabeth said. "Jessica and I only get to see our grandparents on vacations."

"I'd rather go into town with Mom and Dad," Ann said. "I hate the reservation."

Elizabeth stopped brushing. "Hate it? Why?"

"I think all of this Indian stuff is dumb," Ann said. "My favorite things are baseball and computers. At least there's a great computer at the reservation school."

"Why can't you like computers and baseball *and* the reservation?" Elizabeth asked.

Ann sighed. "Because all of the tourists who come to the reservation expect me to sleep in a tepee and do rain dances."

Elizabeth felt her face grow hot. *She* was one of the tourists Ann was talking about. Tepees and rain dances were just what she had expected.

"I don't want to be Water Lily," Ann said. "I just want to be Ann. I don't want to be a Native American. I just want to be a normal kid."

"No way!" Elizabeth said. "Living on the reservation is great. Being a normal kid is boring. You're special."

"My parents won't even buy a TV," Ann argued. "Lots of people on the reservation have them. But my grandfather says television is bad, and my parents don't want to upset him. I'm glad we have horses, or I'd go crazy."

Elizabeth shook her head. She didn't understand. She thought Ann was lucky to live in a place so rich in history.

"What's your house like?" Ann asked.

Elizabeth shrugged. "It's just a regular house. We have a pool and a TV. Jessica and I share a bedroom."

"That sounds great," Ann said with a sigh.

"Maybe you can come visit us someday," Elizabeth said.

"Really? I've never been to California," Ann told her.

The girls were quiet for a few seconds.

"I have an idea," Ann spoke up. "We

could be pen pals. I could write you letters on the computer at school."

Elizabeth smiled. "That sounds great. I love to write."

CHAPTER 7

A Fight!

Jessica opened the stable door two hours later.

"Elizabeth!" Jessica yelled, rushing inside. "Are you still here?"

Ann peeked her head out from a stall. "She's taking a riding lesson."

"Really?" Jessica couldn't believe Elizabeth had been brave enough to get up on such a huge animal. "On a horse?"

Ann laughed. "Of course! She'll be finished soon."

"I'm finished now," Elizabeth said.

She came in from the ring in back. She looked happy.

"Liz, guess what?" Jessica said. "I met a storyteller. He knows lots of great stories from long ago. And he gave me an eagle feather!" She held it up.

Elizabeth stepped closer to look at it. "That's the best souvenir," she said. "I'd like to hear him tell stories, too."

Jessica smiled. She knew her sister would be impressed. Elizabeth loved stories.

"He was great," Jessica said. She turned to Ann. "Do you know Gray Eagle? Is he the chief of your tribe?"

"Chief?" Ann said with a little laugh. "You just said he was a storyteller. How could he be both?"

Jessica shrugged. "I don't know. But he's terrific."

"I know him," Ann said. "He's my grandfather."

"Really?" Jessica asked. "That's excellent!"

"If you say so," Ann said. "He's just a stupid old man. I don't pay attention to him."

"Why?" Elizabeth asked. "He sounds super."

"All he's interested in is Indians," Ann said. "*Bo*-ring."

Jessica felt herself getting angry. How could Ann be so mean? Jessica knew Gray Eagle must feel bad that his granddaughter thought he was stupid.

"I think you're the one who's stupid," Jessica told Ann.

"Me? You don't know anything," Ann yelled. "Just mind your own business." She stomped off, looking furious.

49

Jessica turned to Elizabeth. "What's wrong with her?"

"Well . . ."

Elizabeth explained how Ann felt about the reservation. It made Jessica wish she hadn't shouted at her. But she still thought Ann was wrong. Ann should have been proud Gray Eagle was her grandfather. Jessica was certainly proud to have met him.

CHAPTER 8

A Wise Friend

On Saturday Elizabeth took two more riding lessons. Her instructor said she was doing very well. But the competition was the next day and Elizabeth wanted to practice. She headed to the stables in the late afternoon. When she arrived, Ann was there.

"Hi," Elizabeth said.

Ann didn't answer.

Elizabeth led Starfire out of her stall. She was surprised that Ann was still angry. Elizabeth wanted to saddle the horse the way her instructor had taught her, but she couldn't lift the saddle. It was too heavy. Ann saw Elizabeth struggling, but she didn't offer to help. Elizabeth was about to quit when an old man appeared.

"Hi, Water Lily," he greeted Ann.

"Hi," Ann said grumpily.

"How's your riding coming?" the man asked.

"Fine," Ann said. "I don't want any help."

"OK." The man moved toward Elizabeth. "I met you at story hour yesterday."

Elizabeth smiled. She knew this must be the storyteller. "That was my twin sister, Jessica," she said. "My name's Elizabeth. Jessica loves the feather you gave her."

"I'm Gray Eagle," the man said. "Do you like to ride?"

"I love it," Elizabeth said. "I had my first lesson yesterday and two more today. Now I want to practice, but I need help saddling Starfire and getting up into the saddle."

"I'll help you," Gray Eagle said. He got the saddle Elizabeth had used earlier and put it on Starfire's back. He fastened the girth securely under the horse's belly. "Now step on this stool for some extra height. I'll watch you get on."

Elizabeth nodded. The horse still looked tall. She tried her best, but she couldn't get up.

"You have the wrong foot in the stirrup," Gray Eagle said. Elizabeth laughed. She switched feet and tried again. This time getting up into the saddle was easy.

Elizabeth glanced at Ann. Ann was pretending to ignore her grandfather, but Elizabeth knew she was watching.

"Don't slouch like that," Gray Eagle told Elizabeth. "Sit up straight. Show the horse you're proud."

Elizabeth sat up as straight as she could.

"Now let's see you walk her," Gray Eagle said.

Elizabeth gave Starfire a tiny squeeze with her legs. The mare headed out the open back door. Gray Eagle followed them into the practice ring.

"Did you know there were no horses in North America until Spanish Conquistadores brought them?" Gray Eagle asked Elizabeth. Elizabeth shook her head. "I'm glad that they did," Gray Eagle said.

"I'm glad, too," Elizabeth said, smiling. She agreed with Jessica. Gray Eagle was a wonderful person.

*   *   *

That evening Elizabeth, Jessica, and their mother were walking toward the shower room. It was time to get dressed for the pow-wow. A pow-wow was a special kind of Native American celebration. There was going to be dancing, singing, and arts and crafts. Lots of the Mojave would be wearing traditional tribal clothes. Sometimes pow-wows lasted a whole week and involved different tribes. This one was going to be only one evening long. "I'm really excited," Jessica said.

"Me too," Elizabeth said. "We're going to see the chief."

"And the medicine man," Mrs. Wakefield said.

After they finished dressing, the Wakefields walked toward a big outdoor fire with chairs around it. Nearby, a table piled with food had been set out under an open tent. The Wakefields filled their plates and found a place to sit.

"Hi," Brave Wolf said, joining them. Around his waist he was wearing a knotted cloth made out of woven willow bark. He had braided sandals on his feet, and his chest was bare.

"Awesome!" Steven said. "I wish I could dress like you."

Ann and Brave Wolf's mom and dad came over to say hello. Their names were Horned Owl and Goldenrod. Goldenrod had long black hair and bangs. Horned Owl's hair was long, too. They were both wearing shirts and jeans. They went to sit with Gray Eagle.

"Water Lily and I are going to perform a dance with our grandfather later," Brave Wolf told the Wakefields.

"Neat," Elizabeth said.

Brave Wolf saw Ann. He motioned her over.

Ann came up, but she didn't look at Elizabeth or Jessica. "What?" she asked Brave Wolf.

"You're not ready," Brave Wolf said. "Why aren't you dressed?"

"I am dressed," Ann said, looking down at her shorts and T-shirt.

"That's not what I mean," Brave Wolf said. "We have to dance in ten minutes, and you're suppose to wear your long buckskin dress and your beaded necklaces. Hurry and go change."

"No," Ann said.

"You have to," Brave Wolf insisted.

When Ann didn't move, Brave Wolf rushed over to Gray Eagle and whispered something in his ear. The two of them came back together. But before Gray Eagle could say anything, Ann yelled, "I don't want to dance! I hate pow-wows! I hate those stupid clothes! And I hate *you*!"

Then she turned and ran off.

Elizabeth and Jessica looked at each other. They both knew that things between Ann and Gray Eagle were getting worse. Something had to be done.

CHAPTER 9

The Competition

"Are you nervous?" Mrs. Wakefield asked Elizabeth on Sunday.

"I would be," Jessica said.

It was almost time for the riding competition. Most of the guests were gathered on the bleachers next to the ring. Donny Kale was sitting on Red Sand's lap. Donny's mother was next to them, with the Wakefields on her other side. Steven and Brave Wolf sat in the last row.

"I'm not nervous," Elizabeth said. "I know I won't win. Luke has been taking lessons for a while, and Ann has been practicing for months."

The competition was broken up into age groups. In the group of kids under eight years old, only Ann, a boy named Luke Egan, and Elizabeth were participating.

"Just do your best," Mr. Wakefield said.

"I will," Elizabeth said. "See you later."

Jessica sat on the ground in front of her parents' seats. She watched Elizabeth run off toward the stable. She saw Gray Eagle whisper something into Elizabeth's ear.

Jessica knew Gray Eagle had given her sister lots of advice about what to do during the competition. It looked as if he were giving her some last-minute tips.

Moments later Gray Eagle motioned for the crowd's attention. "These are the rules of the competition," he announced. "Each rider has to lead their horse out of the stable and past the judges. Then they have to stop the horse, get on, and walk the horse around in a circle. My granddaughter will go first."

Ann came out, leading Amber. She looked nervous. When it came time for Ann to mount the horse, Amber took a step sideways. Ann tried to get up again. Again Amber stepped sideways.

"Whoa, girl," Ann muttered.

When Ann tried a third time, the same thing happened.

Donny laughed. "The horse is trying to get away!"

"Shhh," Jessica said. But she had to admit it *was* kind of funny.

On her fourth try, Ann got up. The rest of her performance went well.

Luke did well, too. But he was a bit

of a show-off. Instead of walking his horse, he trotted her.

Elizabeth came out last. She was leading Starfire. Jessica waved to her. Elizabeth smiled. She seemed relaxed. Jessica thought that was because Elizabeth didn't think she could win. She did everything just right.

"That was perfect," Jessica whispered to her mother.

"She looked like a pro," Mrs. Wakefield whispered back.

It was the older group's turn. When they finished, Gray Eagle came forward. "Good job, everyone. I have a ribbon for each child who participated."

Gray Eagle gave out the ribbons. Then he announced the winners in each age group. Elizabeth had won!

Jessica ran over and gave Elizabeth a big hug. Mrs. Wakefield took her pho-

tograph next to Starfire. Elizabeth looked happy and surprised.

Ann looked mad. "I don't understand how you could have won," she came over and told Elizabeth. "I've been riding for months. You've been riding only for a few days. Brave Wolf will never let me forget this."

"I won only because Gray Eagle helped me," Elizabeth said. "He knows tons about horses."

Ann glanced toward Gray Eagle. When she saw he was looking at *her*, she turned her eyes away.

"Maybe Gray Eagle's not as stupid as you think," Jessica whispered.

"I know he isn't," Ann whispered back. "But I've been mean to him for a long time. He'll never forgive me now."

The twins exchanged glances.

"Yes, he will," Elizabeth said. "All you have to do is say you're sorry."

"Do you really think so?" Ann asked.

Jessica nodded. "Yes! And we'll even help you."

CHAPTER 10

Peace Pact

"Come on, kids," Mrs. Wakefield called a few minutes later. "We have only a little while before lunch. We have to pack up the tents and get ready to go."

"We'll be there in a second," Elizabeth called back.

"Come with us," Jessica suggested to Ann. "We'll work on a plan while we pack."

"All right," Ann agreed.

A little over an hour later, all of the Wakefields' belongings were in the station wagon.

"That was hard work," Elizabeth said.

"I'm ready for lunch," Jessica said, wiping her forehead.

Ann bit her lip. "I guess I'm ready, too."

The twins had helped Ann decide what to say to Gray Eagle. But she still looked a little nervous.

After eating a picnic lunch, all of the visitors sat in a circle and listened to Gray Eagle tell story after story.

"I have finished," he said after the last one. "Would anyone else like to tell one?"

Elizabeth poked Ann.

"Now," Jessica whispered.

Ann got up and stepped forward. "I would."

Gray Eagle looked surprised. "Speak, child," he said with a nod of his head.

Ann took a deep breath.

"Once upon a time," she began, her voice shaking a tiny bit, "there lived a Mojave girl who did not honor her grandfather. No one on the reservation could believe one so foolish was descended from one so wise.

"The Mojave didn't know that the girl's ears were closed. When her grandfather spoke, she couldn't hear his beautiful words.

"But then two pale-headed visitors came from the west. They blew into the girl's ears and helped her hear. After that she loved her grandfather more than any other child on the reservation."

Ann's eyes were filled with tears.

Gray Eagle was crying, too. "Water Lily," he said, "you will grow up to be a great storyteller someday."

Ann ran to give her grandfather a hug. "I'm sorry," she whispered to him.

"Let us forget and move on," Gray Eagle said. He patted Ann's hair. "If you like, I will teach you all the stories I know," he added. "You could make your ancestors proud."

Ann smiled. "I'd like that."

Elizabeth leaned over to Jessica. "We did it," she whispered. Jessica squeezed her hand.

"And now it's time for us to say good-bye," Mr. Wakefield told them.

"We have to go," Elizabeth said as she and Jessica walked over to Ann and Gray Eagle. "Thanks for the help with my riding."

"Thanks for the stories," Jessica said.

Ann gave Jessica and Elizabeth each a hug. "Thank you!"

"You're welcome," Jessica said, grinning.

"Do you have our address?" Elizabeth asked Ann. "Don't forget that we're going to be pen pals."

"I have it," Ann said. "And I haven't forgotten."

Brave Wolf, Steven, and Mr. and Mrs. Wakefield joined them.

"Maybe your new friends can come and visit Sweet Valley someday," Mrs. Wakefield said.

"All right," Brave Wolf said.

"Yeah!" Ann shouted.

"That would be great," Jessica and Elizabeth said at the same time.

After school one day the following week, Elizabeth and Jessica found a surprise waiting for them. "Look at what the mailman brought you," Mrs.

Wakefield said as she opened the door. She handed Elizabeth an envelope. "Come eat your snack when you're finished," she added before heading toward the kitchen.

"It's a letter from Ann," Elizabeth said, reading the return address.

"Open it!" Jessica told her.

Elizabeth ripped open the envelope and started to read the letter.

"What does it say?" Jessica asked.

"Ann says she and Gray Eagle have been going riding together every day," Elizabeth said. "She says she's learned a lot from him already. It's signed Water Lily!"

Jessica smiled. "I'm happy they're going to be friends." She peered over Elizabeth's shoulder. "P.S. Starfire says Hi," she read. "That's silly. Everyone knows horses can't talk."

Elizabeth sighed. "Ann, I mean, Water Lily, is so lucky. She gets to ride every day."

Jessica wrinkled her nose. "I don't think she's lucky at all. She has to clean out smelly stalls every day, too."

"I wouldn't mind cleaning out stalls if it meant I got to ride," Elizabeth said.

"You're crazy," Jessica said.

Elizabeth stuck her tongue out at Jessica. "Am not!"

Will Elizabeth get to ride a horse again? Find out in Sweet Valley Kids #45, ELIZABETH'S PIANO LESSONS.

SIGN UP FOR THE SWEET VALLEY HIGH® FAN CLUB!

Hey, girls! Get all the gossip on Sweet Valley High's® most popular teenagers when you join our fantastic Fan Club! As a member, you'll get all of this really cool stuff:

- Membership Card with your own personal Fan Club ID number
- A Sweet Valley High® Secret Treasure Box
- Sweet Valley High® Stationery
- Official Fan Club Pencil (for secret note writing!)
- Three Bookmarks
- A "Members Only" Door Hanger
- Two Skeins of J. & P. Coats® Embroidery Floss with flower barrette instruction leaflet
- Two editions of *The Oracle* newsletter
- Plus exclusive Sweet Valley High® product offers, special savings, contests, and much more!

Be the first to find out what Jessica & Elizabeth Wakefield are up to by joining the Sweet Valley High® Fan Club for the one-year membership fee of only $6.25 each for U.S. residents, $8.25 for Canadian residents (U.S. currency). Includes shipping & handling.

Send a check or money order (do not send cash) made payable to "Sweet Valley High® Fan Club" along with this form to:

SWEET VALLEY HIGH® FAN CLUB, BOX 3919-B, SCHAUMBURG, IL 60168-3919

NAME_____
(Please print clearly)

ADDRESS_____

CITY_____ STATE _____ ZIP_____
(Required)

AGE_____ BIRTHDAY_____ / _____ / _____

Offer good while supplies last. Allow 6-8 weeks after check clearance for delivery. Addresses without ZIP codes cannot be honored. Offer good in USA & Canada only. Void where prohibited by law.
©1993 by Francine Pascal   LCI-1383-123

☎

1 (800) I LUV BKS!

If you'd like to hear more about your
favorite young adult novels and writers . . .
OR
If you'd like to tell us what you thought
of this book or other books
you've recently read . . .

CALL US at 1(800) I LUV BKS
[1(800) 458-8257]

You'll hear a new message about books and
other interesting subjects each month.

**The call is free to you, but please get
your parents' permission first.**